who are you REALLY?

25 Fun Quizzes to Help You Find Out!

By Catherine Daly-Weir

Grosset & Dunlap • New York

P9-CIV-411

Copyright © 1996 by Catherine Daly-Weir. All rights reserved. Published by Grosset & Dunlap, Inc., which is a member of The Putnam & Grosset Group, New York. GROSSET & DUNLAP is a trademark of Grosset & Dunlap, Inc. Published simultaneously in Canada. Printed in the U.S.A.
ISBN 0–44841137–7   A B C D E F G H I J

TABLE OF CONTENTS

Embarrassing Moments:
  What Would You Do? 3
How Honest Are You? 7
How Well Does Your Best Friend
  Really Know You? 11
How Self-Confident Are You? 12
Are You Psychic? 15
Were You Born To Be Wild? 16
Family Matters 19
Are You a People Person? 20
Money Matters 23
Are You a Wimp? 27
Are You a Guy Magnet? 32
Sweet Dreams 35
Are You a Control Freak? 36
Are You Too Self-Centered? 39
Temper, Temper! 43
Do You Have a Big Mouth? 46
Colors 48
Are You a Hopeless Romantic? 49
How Competitive Are You? 52
Fair-Weather or True-Blue . . .
  What Kind of Friend Are You? 55
How (Dis)Organized Are You? 58
Your Divided Brain 60
When Is Tact the Best Tactic? 61
Superstition Smarts 65
Are You Spoiled Rotten? 68
Are You a Leader? 70
The Name Game 73
Let's Get Physical 74
Miss Manners 76
Who's Your Mr. Right? 79

EMBARRASSING MOMENTS:
What Would You Do?

You walk out of the bathroom with toilet paper stuck to your shoe. You forget to pull up your zipper. You slip and fall in the cafeteria, letting the entire school know you wear pink panties with the days of the week embroidered on them (well, hopefully not!). Embarrassing things happen to the best of us. It's how we react that counts. Determine your embarrassment quotient by taking this quiz.

1 **You show up at the big dance wearing the dress of your dreams. One of a kind. You're in seventh heaven. That is, until you run into your mirror image—a girl from your art class is wearing the exact same dress. What would you do?**

(a) Be sure to be on the other side of the room from her at all times.

(b) Pay somebody to spill purple punch all over her. *Now* your dresses are different!

(c) Laugh and make sure to be in a couple of pictures with her. You'll definitely be in the yearbook now!

2 **You are daydreaming in math class, and the teacher calls on you. When you finally realize it, a full two minutes later, the class is in hysterics. The teacher asks what had you so enthralled. Your reaction is to:**

(a) Laugh sheepishly and apologize.

(b) Turn a deep shade of red and run out of the room.

(c) Reply, "Please forgive me, but I was lost in thought about the intricacies of least common denominators."

3 This time you've actually fallen asleep in class with your head on the desk and the imprint of your spiral notebook pressed into your cheek. Worse yet, a glistening string of drool connects your mouth to the desk. When you wake up, the teacher has not noticed, but that very cute guy from the school newspaper certainly has. You:

(a) Yawn, stretch, wipe your mouth, and say, "Excellent power nap."

(b) Smile and shrug.

(c) Never, ever look at him again—as long as you live.

4 You are meeting your boyfriend's parents for the first time. It's going great, and they really seem to like you. Then, while you are eating hors d'oeuvres in the living room, disaster strikes. You accidentally spill cocktail sauce on the immaculate white couch. No one has noticed. What do you do?

(a) Go upstairs to the bathroom and cry.

(b) Say "Oops," ask for a sponge, and start scrubbing.

(c) Cover the mess with a strategically placed throw pillow, then take your boyfriend aside and ask him to clean it up while no one's looking.

5 You're talking to that cute guy from your music class, when he suddenly tells you you've got lettuce stuck between your teeth. You:

(a) Say, "Oh good, now I won't forget what I had for lunch."

(b) Cover your mouth with your hand and keep talking.

(c) Turn purple and run out of the cafeteria in a frantic search for dental floss.

6 You're sitting in the bleachers, watching a pretty boring basketball game. Suddenly you realize that the hunka-hunka-burning love of your dreams is waving at you and mouthing some-thing. You wave back, and motion that you can't understand what he's saying. He motions you to join him. As you start to get up, you suddenly real-ize that he was waving to the girl next to you. How do you react?

(a) Try and save face by motioning to an imaginary person three rows behind him.

(b) Leave. Immediately. Do not pass Go. Do not col-lect $200.

(c) Laugh. What else can you do?

7 You call your boyfriend's house and, thinking that the male voice that answers is his, purr, "Do you know that you are the sexiest man alive?" When his father replies, "This is Mr. Davis," you answer:

(a) "Well...is the second-sexiest man alive home?"

(b) Click. You hang up then and every other time he answers the phone.

(c) "Sorry, Mr. Davis. Could I please speak to Matthew?"

8 You really want a mountain bike. Your well-mean-ing, but completely clueless dad comes home with a bright pink three-speed with a banana seat and one of those white plastic baskets with the flow-ers on it. What do you do?

(a) Insist he remove it from the premises immediately. You'd rather die than be seen on the goofiest bike ever created.

(b) Ride it anyway. If you can keep a straight face, maybe pretty soon everyone will be wanting one.

(c) Complain about it constantly until your father shells out the bucks for the real thing.

SCORING:

(1)	a=2	b=3	c=1
(2)	a=2	b=3	c=1
(3)	a=1	b=2	c=3
(4)	a=3	b=1	c=2
(5)	a=1	b=2	c=3
(6)	a=2	b=3	c=1
(7)	a=1	b=3	c=2
(8)	a=3	b=1	c=2

If your score is:

20 - 24: BEET RED.
You are extremely sensitive to embarrassment. Just remember that stupid things happen to everyone from time to time. You just call more attention to yourself when you overreact.

13 - 19: FAINTLY FLUSTERED.
You get embarrassed now and then—most of us do—but you seem to understand when to take yourself seriously and when to just shrug it off.

8 - 12: CUCUMBER COOL.
What will it take to embarrass you? You have a great attitude and the wonderful ability to laugh at yourself.

HOW HONEST ARE YOU?

Is your motto "Honesty is the best policy," or "The end justifies the means"? Take this quiz and discover how honest you really are.

1 A big English paper is due, and you completely forgot about it 'til the night before. You haven't even finished reading the book. You:

(a) Tell the teacher you've been busy all week nursing your sick dachshund and you need more time.

(b) Grab those *Cliff Notes* and start writing.

(c) Explain that it slipped your mind and ask for an extension, knowing you'll get a lower grade.

2 Your sister borrows your favorite jacket. When she returns it, there's a five dollar bill in the pocket. You:

(a) Return it to her.

(b) Buy yourself some magazines. Finders keepers!

(c) Leave two-fifty on her dresser. After all, the money *could* have been yours, too.

3 You're at a fast food place, and to your surprise the cashier gives you change for a twenty. You're almost positive you only gave her a ten. You:

(a) Give it back.

(b) Convince yourself it must have been a twenty.

(c) Keep it. What comes around goes around.

4 You studied for the science test, but you just can't remember that one little formula. If you move your head to a certain angle, you can see the smartest girl in the class's test. What do you do?

(a) You'd never look. Cheating is wrong.

(b) You don't look. It would be so embarrassing if you got caught.

(c) $E=mc^2$. Excellent!

5 You're at a birthday party, and they're making everybody play a lame blindfold game. But the prize is movie passes, so you go along. The blindfold isn't on straight, and you can see. You:

(a) Peek—a little.

(b) Close your eyes so the game is fair for everyone.

(c) Pin the tail right on that donkey's butt. You're going to the movies!

6 You borrow one of your mother's favorite rings without asking and a stone falls out. You take it to the jeweler's to get it fixed. The next day your mom asks if you've seen it. You answer:

(a) "What ring?"

(b) "I might have it, let me look around," to desperately try and buy yourself some time.

(c) "I confess!"

7 You're a waitress at the Burger Barn and you despise it with the white-hot intensity of a thousand suns. When some customers get up to leave, you spy a ten dollar bill under their table. You:

(a) Pick it up and put it in a safe place. If it was theirs, they'll come back for it. If they don't, it's yours.

(b) Stick it in your pocket. They gave you a lousy tip anyway.

(c) Follow them to the parking lot and return the money.

8 You're at your grandmother's house checking out this rather ugly ceramic vase you know she really likes. While you're putting it back on the shelf, it slips to the floor and breaks. You:

(a) Glue it back together, hoping she won't notice. (Hey, her eyes are going—it could happen!) If she does notice, you'll explain.

(b) 'Fess up immediately.

(c) Leave it where it fell. She'll think her cat broke it.

9 You order some clothing from a mail-order catalog. When the package arrives, you find they've sent you *two* of everything. You:

(a) Return the stuff immediately. You didn't pay for it, so it doesn't belong to you.

(b) Keep it but feel really guilty.

(c) Sell it at your family's next garage sale.

10 You and some friends are going to see a hot new band. One girl couldn't get a ticket and comes up with a plan: She will wait outside for you to bring her someone else's ticket stub. You:

(a) Give her the ticket, but you still think it's wrong.

(b) Give her the ticket, no problem.

(c) Don't do it—it's the same as stealing!

11 True or false:

(a) I have never sneaked into a second movie at the multiplex.

(b) I never screen my calls to avoid talking to someone.

(c) I sometimes have my parents tell unwanted visitors I'm not home when I really am.

12 You're playing a game with friends, and it's down to the final question. If your team answers correctly, you'll win. You realize you had the same question the last time you played with your family. What do you do?

(a) Ask for a new question. You hate to win unfairly.

(b) Pretend to think for a moment, then give the correct answer. Winning *is* everything.

(c) Give your team a hint, but not the whole answer.

13 You have a few friends over on a Friday night. The next day you notice that someone has left a great pair of earrings behind. What do you do?

(a) Phone around until you find their rightful owner.

9

(b) Wear them over the weekend. You'll return them on Monday.

(c) Give your friend a blank look when she asks if you found her earrings.

SCORING:

(1)	a=1	b=2	c=3
(2)	a=3	b=1	c=2
(3)	a=3	b=2	c=1
(4)	a=3	b=2	c=1
(5)	a=2	b=3	c=1
(6)	a=1	b=2	c=3
(7)	a=2	b=1	c=3
(8)	a=2	b=3	c=1
(9)	a=3	b=2	c=1
(10)	a=2	b=1	c=3
(11)	a - true=2	false=0	
	b - true=2	false=0	
	c - true=0	false=2	
(12)	a=3	b=1	c=2
(13)	a=3	b=2	c=1

If your score is:

33 - 42: HONEST ABE.
No question about it, honesty is *your* policy. You have a firm belief in sticking to the truth and nothing can tempt you to behave otherwise. Abe would be proud of you.

22 - 32: STORYTELLER.
You're usually a straight shooter but sometimes you talk yourself into inventing a story or telling a fib. Watch yourself.

12 - 21: LIAR, LIAR, PANTS ON FIRE!
Have you no shame? You can tell a bold-faced lie without batting an eyelash. It's time to rethink the way you've been doing business lately. All lies and no truth makes you a very dishonest girl!

HOW WELL DOES YOUR BEST FRIEND *REALLY* KNOW YOU?

Did you ever wonder how well someone really knows you? Get a piece of paper and answer the following questions. Then get a friend to write down the answers she thinks *you* would give. Find out if she's really been paying attention! You can also try this out on your sister, boyfriend, mom, or dad. Discover who knows you the best—the results may surprise you!

1 If I was marooned on a desert island, the one book I would want to have with me is:

2 My favorite color is:

3 I would never, ever leave the house without my:

4 I often dream of:

5 My favorite outfit is:

6 If my house were on fire and I could save only one thing, it would be (not a person or pet):

7 The cartoon character I most identify with is:

8 My childhood best friend was named:

9 True or false: I had an imaginary friend when I was little. Bonus points: His/her name was:

10 If I had to choose a last meal, it would be:

11 True or false: I believe in kissing on the first date.

12 I have never uttered these words aloud, but much to my surprise I actually find _____ very attractive.

HOW SELF-CONFIDENT ARE YOU?

Do you think you're number one, the bottom of the barrel, or somewhere in between?

1 Your teacher really likes the sculpture you did for your three-dimensional art class and praises you profusely. Your reaction is:
(a) "Thank you very much."
(b) Matter of fact. Of course your artwork is wonderful.
(c) To look behind you to make sure she's not talking to someone else.

2 It's the first beach day of the year. You've been working out all winter in anticipation. What do you wear?
(a) You stay home. You're still not in good enough shape to be seen in a bathing suit.
(b) A flattering one-piece.
(c) A skimpy bikini.

3 Tryouts for the school play begin next week. You've always wanted to test your acting skills. What do you do?
(a) Practice, practice, practice before the big day.
(b) Chicken out at the last minute and sign up to paint the scenery.
(c) Go in cold to your audition. No need to worry— you're sure you'll get the lead.

4 You're dancing with your cousin at a family wedding, when suddenly you realize the dance floor has cleared and all eyes are on the two of you. You:

(a) Use the opportunity to showcase those new lambada steps you've been practicing. Who can resist the "Forbidden Dance"?

(b) Hope that they're not playing the extended dance mix.

(c) Stop in your tracks.

5 You have a crush on a guy in your history class. When you glance up and see him staring at you, you think:

(a) I wonder if he likes me.

(b) Something must be hanging out of my nose.

(c) Another one bites the dust.

6 You've just finished taking a test you studied really hard for. Lots of kids are still working. What do you do?

(a) Drop it right on the teacher's desk. You're sure you got 100%.

(b) Go over each and every answer. You must have made a mistake somewhere.

(c) Double-check some of the more difficult questions.

7 During homeroom there's an announcement over the loudspeaker for you to report to the principal's office—pronto. What's running through your mind?

(a) The principal found out you didn't finish your math homework last night, and you're being suspended.

(b) You must have been nominated for some honor.

(c) You hope it's good news, but you're a little nervous nonetheless.

SCORING:

(1)	a=2	b=3	c=1
(2)	a=1	b=2	c=3
(3)	a=2	b=1	c=3
(4)	a=3	b=2	c=1
(5)	a=2	b=1	c=3
(6)	a=3	b=1	c=2
(7)	a=1	b=3	c=2

If your score is:

17 - 21: I'M FABULOUS.

Are you really that sure of yourself? If so, you could use a slice of humble pie a la mode. Your head is definitely swelled past the breaking point. Sometimes an overconfident attitude is a sign of hidden insecurity. Could this be the case?

12 - 16: I'M FINE.

Maybe you have doubts now and then, but you never let them get in your way. You are self-assured but you've got a touch of humility, too. And you know how to take a compliment. Take this one: you are definitely a secure person.

7 - 11: I'M PATHETIC.

You could use an ego tune-up. You are probably your own harshest critic. Stop being so hard on yourself, and start being more positive about all you have to offer!

ARE YOU PSYCHIC?

Are psychic powers for real? While many people say no, some scientists believe that certain people do have extrasensory perception, or ESP. So how would you like to test your psychic abilities? You'll need a friend, some props, and an open mind!

1 Sit in a comfortable chair and, if you like, put earplugs in your ears and a blindfold over your eyes. Have a friend go into another room and concentrate on a simple picture in a book. Make sure she focuses on sending the picture to you. See if you receive any images.

2 Get two pads of paper and two pencils. Have your friend go into another room and draw some images (agree on how many beforehand). Sketch what comes to you. See if your pictures are close.

3 Take twenty-five index cards. Pick five different symbols (simple ones, like a square, a circle, a sun, a triangle, etc.) and draw a symbol on each card. Then have a friend hold up the cards, one at a time, and concentrate on the image. Number a piece of paper from one to twenty-five, sit across the room, and write down the symbol you think she is looking at as she studies each card. If you have more than five correct, you may have a bit of psychic ability. But if you get only five or less right, don't worry about it. Studies show that ESP abilities seem to come and go. You may just be having an off day.

So how did you do? According to some believers, everyone has psychic capabilities but certain people are better able to put their powers to use. Are you one of them?

WERE YOU BORN TO BE WILD?

Do you boldly go where no girl has gone before, or do you prefer to stay at home and file your nails? Do you like the exciting and unknown, or the tried and true? Are you a wild child, or a stick-in-the-mud? Take this quiz and find out!

1 You're at the movie theater, and there are three films starting in exactly two and a half minutes. You've never heard of any of them and you have to choose quickly. Which one do you go see?

(a) *The Look of Love.*

(b) *Thirty-two Cents: The History of the Postage Stamp.*

(c) *The Curse of the Bloodsucking Leeches in Eye-Popping 3-D.*

2 Your favorite ride at the amusement park is the:

(a) Roller coaster.

(b) Merry-go-round.

(c) Ferris wheel.

3 What is the most daring thing you've ever done?

(a) Asking a guy out without knowing if he liked you back.

(b) Bungee jumping.

(c) Wearing white pants before Memorial Day.

4 When you eat out, you always order:

(a) A hamburger and french fries—maybe onion rings if you're feeling a bit wild.

(b) The most exotic entree—even if it's octopus or alligator.

(c) Something different—as long as the main ingredient is chicken.

5 True or false:
Every night before you go to bed, you lay your clothes out, down to your socks and underwear.

6 A friend invites you to go to a party with her. She'll be the only person you'll know for sure, and she is going to be a little late. She suggests meeting you there. Your reaction:
(a) "I'll meet you on the corner."
(b) "I don't think so—I'll be at your house."
(c) "Fine. We'll rendezvous at the punch bowl."

7 It's that time of year again—oral report season. Your teacher asks who wants to go first. What do you do?
(a) Raise your hand. You love oral reports!
(b) Raise your hand. If you go first, you'll get the dreaded event over with.
(c) Raise your hand? Not when there's the outside chance that the world could end before the last student is done and you'll never get called on!

8 You're in line at the cafeteria behind the cutest guy in school. Here's your chance to make him notice you. What do you do?
(a) Say "Excuse me," and reach for something behind him, giving what you hope is a devastating smile.
(b) Tap him on the shoulder and ask him if he can recommend anything on the menu.
(c) Don't say a word—you don't want to make a fool of yourself!

9 If you had to choose one of these careers, it would be:
(a) Certified Public Accountant.
(b) International spy.
(c) Fashion designer.

10 You're at a school assembly. The featured performer is a hypnotist. She asks for volunteers. What do you do?

(a) Run up onstage. If anyone is going to cackle like a chicken and lay an egg in front of their peers, it's going to be you.

(b) Go up if all your friends go too.

(c) Sink as far down in your seat as you can go. You'd rather die than be onstage in front of the entire student body.

11 You're hanging at the pool with some friends. Someone bets you ten bucks you won't dive off the high board. What do you do?

(a) Climb up, take one look, and do a cannonball.

(b) Say, "You would be correct."

(c) A beautiful swan dive, collecting your ten to thunderous applause.

SCORING:

(1)	a=2	b=1	c=3
(2)	a=3	b=1	c=2
(3)	a=2	b=3	c=1
(4)	a=1	b=3	c=2
(5)	true=0	false=2	
(6)	a=2	b=1	c=3
(7)	a=3	b=2	c=1
(8)	a=2	b=3	c=1
(9)	a=1	b=3	c=2
(10)	a=3	b=2	c=1
(11)	a=2	b=1	c=3

If your score is:

26 - 32: WILD CHILD.

Bungee jumping before breakfast? No question, girl, you live life in the fast lane. Is there anything you won't try? Just keep in mind that sometimes it makes sense to look before you leap.

17 - 25: REASONABLE RISK-TAKER.

Your attitude keeps you right smack in the middle ground, between devil-may-care and playing it safe. You have fun, but you're careful at the same time.

10 - 16: WORRY WART.

You may play it too safe. Learn to throw caution to the wind once in a while. You don't have to go skydiving or parasailing. You can introduce yourself to someone you don't know, go somewhere new—let a little unpredictability into your life.

FAMILY MATTERS

Are you an only child? The baby of the family? Somewhere in the middle? The answer could affect your personality, say some psychologists.

First borns tend to be high achievers and perfectionists. But they may also be cautious and careful.

Middle children often have lots of friends and tend to be quite diplomatic, going out of their way to avoid conflict.

Youngest kids like to be the center of attention and may very well be class clowns. They can be outgoing, and fun to be around.

Only children may be used to getting their own way, and are often loners. They tend to have a good self image.

Of course, many factors besides birth order influence your personality. But you may find some of these descriptions are right on the mark. How do they fit your family?

Do you thrive on the companionship of others, or are your three best friends me, myself, and I? Take this quiz and determine...

ARE YOU A PEOPLE PERSON?

1 **What is your favorite thing to do on a Saturday night?**
(a) Go to a wild party.
(b) Stay in, take a long bubble bath, and read a good book.
(c) Invite a friend or two over and watch some videos.

2 **Which statement best describes your friends?**
(a) A big group of people.
(b) Several good close friends.
(c) I know people from classes and stuff, but there's only one best friend for me.

3 **At a party you:**
(a) Hang with your friends. If you're introduced to someone new, that's cool.
(b) Circulate, introducing yourself to people you don't know.
(c) You don't go to parties. Too much mingling and small talk.

4 **The sport you like most is:**
(a) Tennis.
(b) Volleyball.
(c) In-line skating.

5 **You find family reunions:**
(a) More painful than a bad case of cramps. (If one more person tells you how much you've grown, you think you just might scream!)

(b) Tons of fun. All those relatives in one place!

(c) Enjoyable—but you're glad they're only once a year.

6 You've volunteered to help at your school's alumni reunion. Which committee do you sign up for?

(a) Clean-up—so you won't have to come 'til it's over.

(b) Decorations—so you can have fun with a small bunch of people.

(c) Hospitality—so you can meet and greet everyone involved.

7 Which activity would you be most likely to join at school?

(a) The yearbook, doing layout. You like to work closely with a small group of people.

(b) Nature photography—you, a camera, and the great outdoors.

(c) Cheerleading. There's nothing for you like rallying the entire school to their feet.

8 A girl you've become friendly with at your dance class invites you to hang out with her. She goes to a different school than you, and she wants to introduce you to all her friends. What do you do?

(a) Go—think of all those potential new friends.

(b) Go to make her happy, though you are a bit nervous.

(c) Tell her you've already got plans to stay home and wash your hair.

SCORING:

(1)	a=3	b=1	c=2
(2)	a=3	b=2	c=1
(3)	a=2	b=3	c=1
(4)	a=2	b=3	c=1
(5)	a=1	b=3	c=2
(6)	a=1	b=2	c=3
(7)	a=2	b=1	c=3
(8)	a=3	b=2	c=1

If your score is:

20 - 24: SOCIAL BUTTERFLY.
You love to be surrounded by people (maybe even people you don't know—yet!) and you go out of your way to make new friends. Just keep in mind that sometimes it's okay to go solo—you might enjoy it.

13 - 19: BALANCING ACT.
You divide your time between solo flights and socializing. You like and enjoy other people, but you also know that sometimes there's no better friend than yourself.

8 - 12: THE CHEESE STANDS ALONE.
You are a lone wolf. You prefer solitude to the party scene. Just remember that no woman is an island—we all need a little companionship once in a while.

MONEY MATTERS

Is your nickname "Scrooge"? Do you hoard pennies like they're going out of style? You could be a cheapskate. Or perhaps you are a spendthrift. Does your allowance seem to burn a hole in your pocket? Have you ever considered breaking into your little brother's piggy bank because once again you're short on cash? Take this quiz to determine how you really feel about money.

1 Everyone is chipping in for your homeroom teacher's baby shower gift. You know most people are planning on putting five dollars into the envelope. What do *you* put in?

(a) Six bucks. She's a great teacher.

(b) Five—it's only fair.

(c) Some loose change. There's already enough money to get a decent gift, and no one will ever know.

2 Your best friend moves to another state. How do you keep in touch?

(a) A phone call once a month, along with lots of letters and cards.

(b) You make long distance calls to her whenever the mood hits you.

(c) Out of sight, out of mind. Long distance is sooooo expensive!

3 You're eating out with five friends. Everyone has a burger, fries, and a shake. You have a grilled cheese and a glass of water. When the bill comes:

(a) You split it six ways, as usual. This always happens, but you don't like to make a fuss.

(b) You ask the waitress to make you up a separate check. You're not getting shafted again.

(c) You figure out how much you owe, add the appropriate tip, and hand it over.

4 A girl you're not all that friendly with invites you to her Sweet Sixteen. You give her:

(a) That itchy sweater your Aunt Betty gave you for Christmas. She'll be getting tons of other stuff anyway.

(b) A CD you know she wants.

(c) A pretty expensive gold bracelet. You hate to look cheap.

5 There's a big dance at school in two weeks. You go shopping for a dress. You end up buying:

(a) A dress off the bargain rack—as long as it fits.

(b) The fanciest dress you can find. Maybe you'll be invited to a wedding someday...or a coronation.

(c) Something nice that you'll be able to wear again.

6 It's your little sister's birthday. You know that the biggest treat for her would be for you to take her out for dinner. You go:

(a) To Burger Heaven. Hamburger, fries, shake, and a funny hat for $1.99. What more could a birthday girl ask for?

(b) To a pricey French restaurant. How often does a girl turn nine?

(c) To a fun neighborhood place with good food at reasonable prices.

7 It's your grandmother's seventieth birthday, and there's going to be a big family party. Everyone's getting her something really special. You:

(a) Make your grandmother a scrapbook full of stories, photos, and mementos. It doesn't cost much at all, but it takes a long time and a lot of thought to make.

(b) Sign your name to your parents' gift. Grandma'll never know.

(c) Blow all your savings on a high-priced vase. There are several more family birthdays coming up, but you'll worry about them later.

8 You love in-line skates, but they cost so much. You:

(a) Buy the most expensive, flashy skates around.

(b) Get a nice mid-priced pair.

(c) Borrow your best friend's skates whenever you feel like skating. You're not wasting your money on a fad!

9 One of your friends is having a gathering at her house, and you know she's supplying most of the snacks with her own money. You:

(a) Bring over a six-pack of her favorite soda.

(b) Go wild at the Stop & Pay and bring a whole bagful of different treats. Why not?

(c) Come empty-handed. There will be plenty to go around.

10 You are eating dinner out with a friend. She just got some birthday money and decides to treat, asking you to cover the tip. The bill comes to thirty dollars even. What do you leave for a tip?

(a) Five dollars, maybe six if the service was really good.

(b) Ten dollars. The waiter was really cute.

(c) A buck or two. Maybe they'll just figure your math isn't so great.

11 When you go to the movies, your snack of choice is:

(a) Ice water and popcorn you made at home.

(b) Super Big Swallow Soda, Giant Vat o' Popcorn, and some of those nacho thingies.

(c) Either Twizzlers or Junior Mints, depending on the mood you're in.

SCORING:

(1)	a=1	b=2	c=3
(2)	a=2	b=1	c=3
(3)	a=1	b=3	c=2
(4)	a=3	b=2	c=1
(5)	a=3	b=1	c=2
(6)	a=3	b=1	c=2
(7)	a=2	b=3	c=1
(8)	a=1	b=2	c=3
(9)	a=2	b=1	c=3
(10)	a=2	b=1	c=3
(11)	a=3	b=1	c=2

If your score is:

27 - 33: PENNY PINCHER.
It's good that you're careful with your money—but you may be letting it rule your life. You've got to loosen those purse strings once in a while! Try being a little more open-handed. You just might like it!

18 - 26: EVEN-STEVEN.
You seem to handle money well and always tend to be very fair, whether it's chipping in for something, paying your fair share, or leaving a tip. People appreciate it. Keep up the good spending (and saving) habits.

11 - 17: SPENDAHOLIC.
Be careful—you could be a little too carefree with your hard-earned cash. Take a look at the reasons behind your incredible generosity. Are you trying to show off, or perhaps buy your friends' affections? Your real friends like you for the person you are—not your money.

ARE YOU A WIMP?

Do you let people cut in front of you on line without saying a word? Do you always find yourself doing unto others, while they do not do unto you? Are you on the defensive at all times—knocking people down before they can do it to you? Are you somewhere in the middle? See how you score on the wimp meter.

1 Your best friend has successfully borrowed and lost three pairs of your earrings. She asks to borrow a sweater, and when she returns it, there's a huge ketchup stain on it. You:
(a) Say, "It's okay," and seethe quietly.
(b) Tell her she's a slob and your lending days are over.
(c) Ask her to bring it to the dry cleaner's.

2 You're hanging out with some friends, telling a story about your new cat. A girl rolls her eyes and says, "Oh no, not another Fluffy story," and makes the universal gagging sign. You:
(a) Ignore her.
(b) Laugh, but boil inside.
(c) Say,"Oh that's right, we'd all much rather have you entertain us with yet another tale about your father's expensive new car."

3 You're out on a date with a guy who's just not your type. When he drops you off at your front door, he zooms in for a good-night kiss. Your reaction?
(a) "Back off buddy," and give him a polite handshake.
(b) Offer him the cheek and get inside as quickly as you can.
(c) Kiss him back. You don't want him to feel bad.

4 He asks for a second date. You say:

(a) "Okay," although you're kicking yourself. You'll tell him no next time.

(b) "That's really nice of you, but I don't think it's a good idea."

(c) "No, thanks. I'm just not interested."

5 You just bought a new jacket. It's a little different, but you think it looks really cool. When you wear it to school, a girl passing you by in the hall says, "Nice jacket," in a totally sarcastic voice. You:

(a) Wear it anyway. You like it and that's all that matters.

(b) Hang it in the back of your closet. You'll never wear *that* thing again.

(c) Wear it as often as is humanly possible. You'll show that girl what you think of *her* opinion.

6 In English class you're teamed up with a guy you don't know very well to give an oral report on *Romeo and Juliet.* He proposes a topic: "Romeo, Juliet, Tybalt, and Mercutio: Whose Death Hurt the Most?" You would rather die. What do you do?

(a) Insist on doing a topic you choose, such as "Romeo and Juliet: Teenage Crush or True Love?" knowing he will really hate it.

(b) Go along with him. He's very persuasive.

(c) Choose a new topic together.

7 You're angry with a friend for spending more time with her new boyfriend than with you. When she asks what's wrong, you say:

(a) "To tell you the truth, I'm a little upset with you."

(b) "What's wrong? You're the worst friend in friendship history. *That's* what's wrong."

(c) "Nothing." You're mad, but you're too embarrassed to explain.

8 You are at a little boutique, trying to return a dress you bought. You are being very polite, but the saleswoman is incredibly rude. It's quite obvious that she thinks she can intimidate you because of your age. How do you react?

(a) Say, "Excuse me, but who died and crowned you queen?"

(b) Ask for her name and the name of her manager, then call and lodge a complaint.

(c) Remain polite, leave the store, and think on the way home of a million great remarks you could have made.

9 You have worked for two weeks on a book report and it's a masterpiece. When you get it back from your teacher, you've gotten a good grade, but she's written a note on it implying it's so good all the ideas could not have possibly been yours. How do you react?

(a) Picket her classroom. What a loser!

(b) Explain the situation to her.

(c) You don't say a word. You got the grade you wanted, and besides, you hate to make a fuss.

10 A friend asks to borrow some money for what seems like the millionth time. You're not even sure if she's paid you back from last time. You:

(a) Say, "Sorry, you already cleaned me out."

(b) Give it to her but make her sign an I.O.U.

(c) Fork it over and kiss your lunch money good-bye.

11 You have a half-day at school. The afternoon is yours. You want to go to the beach and catch some rays, but all your friends want to go to the movies. You:

(a) Compromise and go to the mall.

(b) Go to the movies—you hate to disappoint anyone.

(c) Go to the beach alone if you have to—you're not letting anyone else tell you what to do.

12 You're very good at chemistry. Your lab partner hasn't got a clue. When it comes time to do the lab reports, you:

(a) Do all the work, letting him copy all your answers.
(b) Try to encourage him to participate and help you out.
(c) Ask for a new partner. This isn't fair.

13 You and a group of friends all are taking cabs to a party. Just your luck, you end up sharing a cab with "Chintzy Chelsea," the girl who never remembers when it's her turn to pay. When you arrive at your destination, she's not reaching for her cash. You:

(a) Hand her exactly half of the money and get out of the cab.
(b) Pay up. You hate awkward situations.
(c) Pretend you can't find your wallet and force her to cover the entire fare, tip included.

SCORING:

(1)	a=3	b=1	c=2
(2)	a=2	b=3	c=1
(3)	a=1	b=2	c=3
(4)	a=3	b=2	c=1
(5)	a=2	b=3	c=1
(6)	a=1	b=3	c=2
(7)	a=2	b=1	c=3
(8)	a=1	b=2	c=3
(9)	a=1	b=2	c=3
(10)	a=1	b=2	c=3
(11)	a=2	b=3	c=1
(12)	a=3	b=2	c=1
(13)	a=2	b=3	c=1

If your score is:

31 - 39: JELLYFISH.
You are wimpy, wimpy, wimpy! Stop letting people walk all over you. Show some backbone. Hey, you deserve respect as much as anyone else. If you stand up for yourself firmly but politely, you won't spend the next week obsessing over what you "should have" said or done.

22 - 30: STAND-UP GIRL.
Nobody's taking advantage of you, that's for sure. You know how to stand up for yourself, but you see the other guy's side, too. And you don't resort to cruel comebacks or rude retorts—you set people straight in a pleasant manner. That's quite a talent!

13 - 21: TERMINATOR.
You are definitely not a wimp, and you never let people take advantage of you. You set them straight so fast they don't know what hit them! But you sometimes take it too far— there's no need to be nasty.

ARE YOU A GUY MAGNET?

Do the members of the opposite sex flock to you like flies to honey or do they avoid you like the plague? Find out if you are a guy magnet—or what you can do if you would like to be one!

1 You're at the library getting books for your history report. In the reference section you run into a cute guy from your class. He says hello. You:

(a) Get nervous and ramble on about the complexities of the Dewey decimal system.

(b) Convince him to join your history study group—just don't tell him you're the only other member!

(c) Ask about his topic and chat for a while.

2 On a first date, you:

(a) Keep the conversation going, but also ask questions, make jokes, whatever.

(b) Don't talk much—you are afraid of saying something stupid.

(c) Flirt like crazy.

3 A guy in your math class has been absent for a while and he asks to borrow your notes. You:

(a) Give him a big wink as you hand them over. You know what he's really after—you!

(b) Say sure, and tell him to call if he has questions.

(c) Say no, informing him about your policy never to lend out your notes.

4 You are at a crowded party and notice that a guy across the room keeps looking at you. He is a babe and a half. You:

(a) Smile at him, perhaps even walk over and introduce yourself if you're in the mood.

(b) Stroll over and say, "Hey, see anything you like?"

(c) Turn the other way. You hate being stared at!

5 This time you spot a special someone you are interested in. What do you do?

(a) Catch his eye and motion for him to join you.

(b) Admire him all evening—when he's not looking.

(c) Ask someone who knows the both of you to casually introduce you.

6 It's Valentine's Day and you have a crush on someone. What do you do?

(a) Slip a card in his locker reading, "Will You Be My Valentine?" and sign it, "Guess Who."

(b) Slip a card in his locker reading, "Will You Be My Valentine?" with your name and phone number.

(c) It crosses your mind to do something cute—but that would be way too forward.

7 You're at a party that isn't going all that well. It's like there's a line drawn across the room—boys on one side, girls on the other. Do you do anything?

(a) You break the ice by suggesting a game of Spin the Bottle and volunteer to go first.

(b) You get a couple of friends together to make the big move across the room.

(c) Yeah, right.

8 Your parents have hired the cutest guy in the neighborhood to mow your lawn. You:

(a) Put on your bikini, grab a towel, and strategically place yourself in the middle of the lawn.

(b) Offer him a cool glass of lemonade and strike up a conversation.

(c) Stay inside. You might have to talk to him.

9 Describe your typical weekend:

(a) If I have fewer than three dates, I'm crushed.

(b) I have a date, or go out with my friends.

(c) I watch reruns of *Growing Pains* with Mom.

10 You're off to the beach where there are sure to be lots of cute guys. What's your reading material?

(a) Whatever's good and on the best-seller list.

(b) *Football Rules and Regulations: Unabridged.*

(c) *Women Are From Earth, Who Cares Where Men Are From?*

SCORING:

(1)	a=1	b=3	c=2
(2)	a=2	b=1	c=3
(3)	a=3	b=2	c=1
(4)	a=2	b=3	c=1
(5)	a=3	b=1	c=2
(6)	a=2	b=3	c=1
(7)	a=3	b=2	c=1
(8)	a=3	b=2	c=1
(9)	a=3	b=2	c=1
(10)	a=2	b=3	c=1

If your score is:

24 - 30: FEMME FATALE.

You aren't afraid to be bold and make your move. Your forward ways might scare off some of the shyer guys, but they probably aren't your type anyway! Be careful of coming off as too pushy, however.

17 - 23: A FRIENDLY FACE.

You are friendly and easygoing and seem to make guys feel comfortable around you. You probably have lots of friends of both sexes, and perhaps even a special someone, too.

10 - 16: THE INVISIBLE GIRL.

Could it be that guys make you a wee bit nervous? Okay, guys may seem strange sometimes, but they aren't a different species! Guys need a little encouragement now and then—so just relax and try to be a little friendlier!

SWEET DREAMS

*You're walking down the hallway at school. It's full of peo-
ple you know—and they're all laughing and pointing at you.
Suddenly you realize you're as naked as a jaybird. The school
bell starts to ring. You panic—class is about to begin, and
you're out of dress code!* Thankfully the ringing bell is really
your alarm clock. You're in your bedroom, not in school. It
was only a dream. But you start wondering—what did that
strange dream mean? Here are a few common dreams and
some interpretations of them.

**To dream of being naked could mean you feel vul-
nerable, like your faults are being exposed, or
that a secret has come out into the open.**

**To dream of falling probably means you are feel-
ing insecure.**

**To dream of flying could mean that you feel good
about something you've achieved. Or it could signify that you are looking to escape from your
responsibilities.**

**To dream of danger that you can't escape might
mean you are afraid of getting caught for something you've done.**

Of course, just as every dreamer is different, every dream is,
too. Dreams are very personal—most dreams are about
what has happened to us the day before. We can learn a lot
about ourselves by paying close attention to our dreams.
Try keeping a notebook and a pen next to your bed and
write in it as soon as you wake up each morning. You might
have some interesting insights!

Happy Dreaming!

ARE YOU A CONTROL FREAK?

When you played house when you were little, did you insist on being the mother? Do you always have to be the one in charge? Some people just can't stand it when they aren't in total control. Are you one of them?

1 Your friend is making a guest list for a party. She has included the names of some people who are, in your humble opinion, total geeks. You:

(a) Announce, "I won't go if you invite social misfits."

(b) Sigh and say, "If you really find it necessary to ask them, I won't say another word."

(c) Keep your mouth shut. It's her party and none of your business.

2 You're running for class office. A friend offers to help make posters. They're not quite up to your exacting standards. What do you do?

(a) Grin and bear it, then take them home and fix them.

(b) Tell her that her artwork bites the big one and make her start over.

(c) Put them up as is. You're lucky you didn't have to do them all by yourself.

3 Your little brother asks for your help making a diorama for social studies class. It just so happens that you are a diorama expert. You:

(a) Take over. This will be the best diorama ever!

(b) Sit down and discuss the project with him, give him some helpful hints, then leave him be.

(c) Hang around for a while in case he runs into trouble, then jump in.

4 You just got a really cool pair of shoes. Your sister wants the same ones. What is your reaction?

(a) All right—as long as she never wears them on the same days as you.

(b) No way! That would be too embarrassing!

(c) No problemo. You are secure in your individuality.

5 You are baking a cake for your father's birthday. It comes out looking a bit lopsided. You:

(a) Throw it away and vow never to bake again.

(b) Fill in the flat spot with some extra icing. No one will be the wiser.

(c) Put the cake to the side for future snacking and start over. Maybe the next one will be better.

6 A friend is passing around some photos taken at a recent slumber party. To your horror, there's a picture of you in your long johns with the drop seat, and a lampshade on your head. You:

(a) Laugh along with everyone else, saying, "I always knew I was the brightest girl there."

(b) Feel really stupid, but pretend you don't care.

(c) Rip the picture in half and destroy the negative.

7 When things don't go as planned, you:

(a) Freak out.

(b) Enjoy it—just another one of life's little adventures.

(c) Try to fix the situation if at all possible.

8 For your birthday a friend gives you a CD you've never heard of before. What do you do?

(a) Return it immediately for Billboard's #1 album.

(b) Listen to it—hey you might like Cereal Killers.

(c) Keep it, but probably never listen to it.

9 In art class you accidentally spill red paint all over your white shirt. What do you do?

(a) Rush home to soak and bleach.

(b) Put a sweater over it—nobody'll know.

(c) Wear it—it actually looks kinda cool.

10 Your grandmother treats you to lunch—at a Japanese restaurant. She urges you to try the sushi. Your reaction?

(a) Try a bite of hers. It won't kill you.

(b) Order the sushi special.

(c) Pretend to throw up and order the chicken teriyaki. Raw fish for lunch—very funny, Grandma!

SCORING:

(1)	a=3	b=2	c=1
(2)	a=2	b=3	c=1
(3)	a=3	b=1	c=2
(4)	a=2	b=3	c=1
(5)	a=3	b=1	c=2
(6)	a=1	b=2	c=3
(7)	a=3	b=1	c=2
(8)	a=3	b=1	c=2
(9)	a=3	b=2	c=1
(10)	a=2	b=1	c=3

If your score is:

24 - 30: CONTROL QUEEN.
You really like to be in control, but a part of you must know you can't make the whole world run by your rules. Loosen up a bit—sometimes you have the most fun when life throws you a curve ball.

17 - 23: SEMI-STRESSED.
While not officially a "control freak," you may be letting life get to you a little too often. Give your stressed-out half a good pep talk. With a little work you could be practically stress-free!

10 - 16: TAKING IT EASY.
Easygoing is your middle name. You're not afraid to have new experiences, which makes your world bigger. Your live-and-let-live attitude makes you enjoyable to be around. Is there such a thing as being *too* easygoing? Not as long as you're honest with yourself about your feelings.

ARE YOU TOO SELF-CENTERED?

Do people ever tell you that you are selfish? Do they call you an egomaniac? Could they be right? Take this quiz and see!

1 It's the season finale of your favorite TV show. All your friends will be talking about it at school on Monday. Your parents want you to go to your uncle's retirement party. What do you do?

(a) Tape it. You'll watch it later.

(b) Go to the party, but sneak off to a bedroom with a TV. There's nothing like watching it live.

(c) Stay home. Retirement parties are sooooo boring.

2 It's Christmas morning. You just happen to notice that your little brother got two more presents than you did. How do you react?

(a) Sulk all day. 'Tis the season to be cheated.

(b) You're mad, but you keep your mouth shut. After all, it is the season of peace. You'll bring it to your parent's attention when you need the leverage.

(c) It doesn't bother you at all.

3 It's your mom's birthday, and she wants the whole family to go to her favorite Indian restaurant. You despise curry. What do you do?

(a) Go and order something relatively bland. You'll survive.

(b) Go, but refuse to eat a thing.

(c) Insist that chicken tikka gives you the hives and that if she wants you to be at the dinner party, it must be someplace else.

4 Your parents ask you to baby-sit on a Saturday night. You don't have anything planned, so you:

(a) Say, "Sure."

(b) Do it, but make sure your parents know what a sacrifice it is so you get paid big bucks.

(c) Make plans quick. The last thing you want to do on a Saturday night is stay home with your siblings.

5 You are treating your little bro to a movie for his birthday. He wants to go see a low-budget action flick that got two thumbs down. You:

(a) Go see *Fists of Concrete* and bring your earplugs. You could use a couple hours sleep.

(b) Compromise on a nice Disney movie.

(c) Take him to see a romantic comedy. It's never too early for the kid to learn something about *amore*.

6 Your mom baked your favorite dessert—coconut cream pie. There's only one piece left and you've been looking forward to eating it all day. It seems your father has the same idea. You:

(a) Grab it and run.

(b) Let him have the pie—after all, he's worked hard all day.

(c) Split it with him.

7 Your friend ate tuna fish for lunch, and she asks you if you have any gum. You do, but it's your last piece and you were saving it for later. You:

(a) Give her the gum. She needs it more than you do.

(b) Give her half so she doesn't knock anyone over with her fish breath.

(c) Give her a blank look. What gum?

8 Your mom has had a rough day at the office. She's telling you this very involved story that has something to do with a Xerox machine that you have absolutely no interest in. What do you do?

(a) Cut her off, saying, "I'll bet Dad would really love to hear all about this when he gets home."

(b) Begin telling her about your hellish day at school. Hey, you understand where she's coming from!

(c) Listen quietly. You know she just wants to get it off her chest.

9 Your brother is a Civil War buff. He can't tell you enough about it. When he begins another one of his monologues, you:

(a) Say "Uh-huh, uh-huh" over and over again until he's through.

(b) Throw a pillow at him.

(c) Ask him questions even though you've heard it all before.

10 You're out shopping with a friend, when she spots the very dress you've had your eye on for weeks. There's only one left—and it's on sale. She tries it on and it looks great. What do you say when she asks for your opinion?

(a) "I'm not quite sure if red's your color."

(b) "It looks wonderful on you."

(c) "Not bad."

11 You are at the movies with a good friend you haven't seen in a while. You just can't stop talking. The man in the row in front of you turns around and shushes you. You:

(a) Laugh with your friend, but then lower your voices to the occasional whisper.

(b) Immediately shut up. You didn't realize you were being so loud.

(c) Tell him that if he is bothered by you he should change his seat.

12 Your mom is on a serious weight-loss program. How does this affect your eating habits?

(a) You eat the same as usual—ignoring your mother's hungry stare as you chow down on your chocolate chip cookie dough ice cream.

41

(b) You take your snacks to your bedroom for the time being.

(c) You do all your snacking outside the house so your mom won't be tempted by goodies in the cupboard.

SCORING:

(1)	a=1	b=2	c=3
(2)	a=3	b=2	c=1
(3)	a=1	b=2	c=3
(4)	a=1	b=2	c=3
(5)	a=1	b=2	c=3
(6)	a=3	b=1	c=2
(7)	a=1	b=2	c=3
(8)	a=3	b=2	c=1
(9)	a=2	b=3	c=1
(10)	a=3	b=1	c=2
(11)	a=2	b=1	c=3
(12)	a=3	b=2	c=1

If your score is:

29 - 36: IT'S ALL ABOUT YOU.
You seem to think that you are the sun and everyone and everything should revolve around you. Sure, you've got to look out for yourself—but you're going overboard. Snap out of it! Your "me-first" style won't win you any popularity contests.

20 - 28: IT'S A LOT ABOUT YOU.
You aren't the center of your own universe—yet. But with a couple of more rotations, you could be well on your way. Watch out!

12 - 19: WE'RE IN IT TOGETHER.
You should be proud of yourself. You are a thoughtful and considerate person, and you set a stellar example for others to follow.

TEMPER, TEMPER!

What does it take to make your blood boil? Your pulse quicken? Do you get hot under the collar, or are you as cool as a cucumber? Take this quiz and find out how your temper rates.

1 **When you are angry, you:**
(a) Throw things and scream.
(b) Sulk for a while.
(c) Sigh deeply.

2 **You wanted a CD player for your birthday. You get a new sweater instead. How do you react?**
(a) You're disappointed but you try not to show it.
(b) You pout all day.
(c) Tell your mom you didn't really want a CD player anyway—you hear vinyl is making a comeback.

3 **You are in the middle of taking a tough history test when your annoying teacher falsely accuses you of cheating. You:**
(a) Silently hand the test to your teacher (you hate to create a scene), then make an appointment with the principal to give your side of the situation.
(b) Step outside, calmly explain, and ask if you can return to your test because time's a-wasting.
(c) Rip up your test and leave the room.

4 **You are at the movies with some friends, when you spot your boyfriend sitting several rows ahead with a pretty blonde girl. You:**
(a) Walk up behind them, say, "Guess who?" and dump your jumbo popcorn (with extra butter) on his head.
(b) Follow him when he gets up to get a coke, and invite him and his "friend" to sit with you. Just watch him try to squirm his way out of that one!

(c) Forget about it—you are sure there's got to be a reasonable explanation—maybe it's like one of those wacky *Brady Bunch* episodes where she's really just his cousin.

5 During an important soccer match, a player on the other team blatantly fouls you and doesn't get a yellow card. What do you do?

(a) Nothing. You're sure she's just having a bad day.

(b) Take her legs out from under her the next time she goes up for a head ball.

(c) Walk over to her and say, "You are a dirty player. I, on the other hand, rely upon my superior skill."

6 You've been working on a poster for school for several days now. It's finally perfect, so you leave it to dry on the kitchen counter. When you come back an hour later, you find that your cat has walked across it and smudged it. What do you do?

(a) You're a little peeved, but you just add a couple of strategically placed flowers to cover up the smudges.

(b) Rip it into a million pieces and throw kitty's catnip mouse into the garbage.

(c) Sigh and start over.

7 Your boyfriend is supposed to pick you up at 7:30. He pulls up an hour later. You:

(a) Open the door, say, "Drop dead," and slam it in his face.

(b) Throw your arms around him and say, "No need to explain. I'm just glad you're okay."

(c) Give him a chance to offer an explanation. If it's good, maybe you'll still go out with him tonight.

8 It's the first snow day of the year, and you are psyched to be a couch potato all day and catch up on your favorite soaps. You settle in on the couch with a bowl of popcorn and a steaming cup of cocoa and flip on the TV. To your dismay, *The Young and the Reckless* has been preempted by yet another presidential speech. Your reaction is:

(a) To throw your popcorn at the screen and go back to bed.

(b) It really doesn't bother you at all—you've been meaning to catch up on current events.

(c) To watch cartoons and hope the big guy makes it snappy.

SCORING:

(1)	a=3	b=2	c=1
(2)	a=2	b=3	c=1
(3)	a=1	b=2	c=3
(4)	a=3	b=2	c=1
(5)	a=1	b=3	c=2
(6)	a=2	b=3	c=1
(7)	a=3	b=1	c=2
(8)	a=3	b=1	c=2

If your score is:

20 - 24: FIRECRACKER.
Your temper could get you into trouble one of these days! Try to think things through instead of blowing your top the next time you get angry. Nobody likes to be out of control. Do you?

13 - 19: MS. MELLOW.
You seem to have a good handle on your emotions. You get mad when it's called for, but you realize that sometimes you've just got to make the best of a bad situation.

8 - 12: SERENE QUEEN.
Do you ever get angry? You seem almost too calm. Could you be bottling your anger inside? Everyone needs to let off steam once in a while.

DO YOU HAVE A BIG MOUTH?

Can you keep a secret, or do you spill your guts every chance you get? Are you a blabbermouth, or do you firmly believe that a secret is sacred? Take this quiz to determine your gossip rating.

1 Complete this sentence: Gossip is...
(a) All right, as long as it doesn't get too out of hand.
(b) Great fun.
(c) Harmful if swallowed.

2 Complete this sentence: Talk shows are...
(a) The work of the devil.
(b) My life!
(c) Mildly entertaining once in a while.

3 You are at a party. While on line for the bathroom, you run into a girl you know very casually from school. She is quite popular, and you've always been a bit jealous of her. She is very upset about something and drags you into the bathroom and spills her guts to you, making you promise not to tell anyone. Do you?
(a) You share a few juicy tidbits with your friends, but never name names.
(b) No way. A promise is a promise.
(c) Are you kidding? You'd tell the world.

4 You overhear an unflattering story about a girl you don't know. Do you pass it on?
(a) But of course!
(b) You'd try not to, but it might slip out.
(c) Your lips are sealed.

5 Suppose it's about someone you know. Now do you tell?
(a) Of course not.

(b) Maybe—depends on how bad it is.

(c) Certainly. A juicy story is a juicy story.

6 Complete this sentence: If you don't have anything nice to say...

(a) That's okay, but don't share it with me, please!

(b) I'll be your best friend.

(c) Say nothing at all.

7 There's a rumor going around school that you are secretly dating the quarterback of the football team and that his girlfriend is really angry. You are only tutoring him in bio, nothing more, but you do have a little crush on him. Someone asks you point blank if the story is true. You:

(a) Smile mysteriously.

(b) Say, "Well, we have been getting close during our tutoring sessions..."

(c) Deny it, then go to his girlfriend and explain the deal to her.

SCORING:

(1)	a=2	b=3	c=1
(2)	a=1	b=3	c=2
(3)	a=2	b=1	c=3
(4)	a=3	b=2	c=1
(5)	a=1	b=2	c=3
(6)	a=2	b=3	c=1
(7)	a=2	b=3	c=1

If your score is:

17 - 21: BIG MOUTH STRIKES AGAIN!

You couldn't keep a secret if your life depended on it. Have you ever considered a career as a gossip columnist? But seriously, you'd better watch out—once your friends figure out you're a blabbermouth, you may never be taken into anyone's confidence again.

12 - 16: ALL EARS.
You can't deny you enjoy a good bit of gossip every once in a while, but you do try to keep from being nasty. You'd never intentionally harm anyone. But be careful—whether it's intentional or not, gossip can still be very hurtful.

7 - 11: YOUR LIPS ARE SEALED.
You despise gossip and avoid indulging in it. People trust you—they know that their secrets will go no farther than you.

COLORS

Most everyone has a favorite color—fire engine red, sky blue, lemon yellow, peppermint pink. But did you ever stop to think that your favorite color might hold some clues to your personality?

PEOPLE WHO LIKE:	ARE USUALLY:
RED	popular, energetic, persuasive
ORANGE	friendly, out-going
YELLOW	happy, talkative
GREEN	generous, considerate
BLUE	hard-working, industrious
PURPLE	shy, sensitive
PINK	kind, caring
BROWN	sincere, honest, realistic
BLACK	sophisticated, independent, secretive

Bet you didn't know your favorite color said so much about you!

ARE YOU A HOPELESS ROMANTIC?

Do you find yourself humming *Someday My Prince Will Come* while cleaning your room, or do you think that true love is like happy endings—found only in the movies?

1 **True or false:**
There is one perfect mate out there for everyone, and I will find him!

2 **Your favorite holiday is:**
(a) Christmas.
(b) Valentine's Day, of course!
(c) Halloween.

3 **Your idea of the perfect date is:**
(a) Dancing.
(b) A candlelit dinner for two.
(c) Ice fishing.

4 **Your favorite couple of all time is:**
(a) Popeye and Olive Oyl.
(b) Romeo and Juliet.
(c) Beavis and Butthead.

5 **If you had to choose one of the following, it would be:**
(a) True love.
(b) World peace.
(c) A killer bod.

6 **Finish this sentence: I cry at sappy movies...**
(a) Never!

(b) Only when I've had a bad day.

(c) All the time. Hey, I cry at sappy commercials!

7 The best gift my boyfriend could give me would be:

(a) My very own ant farm.

(b) A heart-shaped locket with his picture inside.

(c) Tickets to see my favorite band in concert.

8 Complete this sentence: I like a movie with...

(a) Lots of action.

(b) Thought-provoking issues.

(c) All I ask for is a happy ending.

9 Your boyfriend just broke up with you. What are you thinking?

(a) This is going to take me a while to get over.

(b) If I wait, he'll come back. We were meant to be.

(c) His loss.

10 When you go to the movies with your guy you like to:

(a) Hold hands.

(b) Eat Jujy Fruits.

(c) Discuss it together afterward.

11 What do you look for in a guy?

(a) Nice personality and good sense of humor.

(b) Tall, dark, and handsome.

(c) The XY chromosome and a full set of teeth.

12 My idea of the perfect vacation is:

(a) Mountain climbing in the Himalayas.

(b) Disneyland.

(c) There's nowhere for me but Paris, *naturalment.*

SCORING:

(1)	true=2	false=0	
(2)	a=2	b=3	c=1
(3)	a=2	b=3	c=1
(4)	a=2	b=3	c=1
(5)	a=3	b=2	c=1
(6)	a=1	b=2	c=3
(7)	a=1	b=3	c=2
(8)	a=1	b=2	c=3
(9)	a=2	b=3	c=1
(10)	a=3	b=1	c=2
(11)	a=2	b=3	c=1
(12)	a=1	b=2	c=3

If your score is:

28 - 35: HARLEQUIN HEROINE.
You see the world through rose-colored glasses, that's for sure. You eat, sleep, and dream romance. Just don't get too carried away—everyone needs a reality check once in a while. And whatever you do, make sure your perfect picture of the way a romance *should* be doesn't get in the way of a real relationship.

19 - 27: REASONABLY ROMANTIC.
You seem to have a level-headed view of love—although you aren't above doodling a guy's name in your notebook or indulging in a sappy movie from time to time. You strike a healthy balance between romanticism and reality.

11 - 18: HEART OF STONE.
Do you have ice water running through your veins, or what? Pick some flowers, daydream about that cute guy in your English class. Romance doesn't have to be totally sappy—it can actually be fun!

HOW COMPETITIVE ARE YOU?

Were your first words "Me first"? Do you believe that winning isn't everything, it's the only thing, or are the words "On your mark, get set..." enough to send you running—in the other direction?

1 You are running for class president. Your nasty opponent has a reputation for playing dirty tricks. Your strategy is to:

(a) Go out of your way to say only nice things about him. Win or lose, you'll be the better person.

(b) Run a clean campaign. If he makes any campaign promises you disagree with, you'll bring it up, but there will be no funny business.

(c) Start an all-out, no-holds-barred, mud-slinging campaign, spreading a rumor that he's a secret bed-wetter.

2 You and a good friend are both trying out for spots on the cheerleading squad. You:

(a) Practice together. You are competitors, but still friends.

(b) Decide that if you make it and she doesn't, you will turn down the spot out of loyalty.

(c) Don't even talk to her during the tryouts. You don't want to lose your competitive edge.

3 Your little sister just brought home a straight-A report card. Your parents are ecstatic. Yours was good, but not that good. How do you react?

(a) Say, "Third grade is so easy!"

(b) Tell her, "Wow, you are much smarter than I'll ever be."

(c) Congratulate her on doing so well.

4 Your best friend and her sister are going to the R.E.M. concert. It's sold out, but their father was able to pull some strings. Your reaction:

(a) "Have a great time."

(b) "Big deal. I think they're pretty overrated."

(c) "You are so cool—I'd never be able to get tickets to such a great concert."

5 A good friend of yours just lost a lot of weight. She shows up at your house and tells you she's always dreamed of being able to wear your jeans, and asks if she can try them on. You oblige and are surprised to see that they're kind of big on her. You say:

(a) "Oh, I must have given you my baggy jeans. Why don't you come back when you've really lost some weight?"

(b) "You look wonderful—I'm such a fat pig!"

(c) "Congratulations."

6 A friend who never studies does really well on the PSATs—much better than you, and you study all the time. What's your reaction?

(a) You berate yourself for being so stupid.

(b) You tell yourself it's obviously not much of a test if she's the cream of the crop.

(c) You say, "That's wonderful! Maybe you can give me some pointers before the mother of all standardized tests."

7 One of your friends is bragging about how good she is at tennis, something she knows you have no talent at. You:

(a) Say, "I know, I'm such a klutz when it comes to racquet sports."

(b) Change the subject.

(c) Retort, "Well, at least *I* can dance."

SCORING:

(1)	a=1	b=2	c=3
(2)	a=2	b=1	c=3
(3)	a=3	b=1	c=2
(4)	a=2	b=3	c=1
(5)	a=3	b=1	c=2
(6)	a=1	b=3	c=2
(7)	a=1	b=2	c=3

If your score is:

17 - 21: ON A CRASH COURSE.

Whoa there, pardner! It's clear that you want the best for yourself—and that's great. But you need to realize that everything in life isn't a contest. You may be trampling on other people's feelings more than you realize. Tone it down a bit while you still have friends.

12 - 16: ENJOYING THE RIDE.

You're right in the middle—not too competitive and not too laid back. You know when to give it your all and when to kick back and relax.

7 - 11: ASLEEP AT THE WHEEL.

Quick! Check for a pulse! You're not competitive in the least. In fact, you may even put yourself down to build other people up, and that's not right. Think about it. Don't you get an urge to be out in front sometimes? Hey—a little competition is healthy. Give it a try.

FAIR-WEATHER OR TRUE-BLUE...WHAT KIND OF FRIEND ARE YOU?

There are all kinds of friends—good ones, bad ones, in-between ones. Which best describes you? Think about it—are you the kind of friend you'd want to have for yourself?

1 A guy you've had a crush on for what seems like forever asks you to go out on Saturday night. You've already told your best friend you'll hang with her to discuss her latest boyfriend woes. You:

(a) Tell him yes—your friend will understand.

(b) Tell him you'll call and let him know. Then explain the situation to your friend. It's up to her.

(c) Reschedule. Your friend needs you.

2 The above situation is reversed. Your friend asks you what she should do. You:

(a) Tell her it's okay, but feel let down. Some best friend!

(b) Tell her it's okay and mean it. At least one of you has a date!

(c) Tell her she has to be there for you—she promised!!

3 When you get to school on Monday morning, rumors are flying fast and furious about a good friend of yours. Apparently she made a major fool out of herself at a party on Saturday night. How do you react?

(a) Find your friend—fast. Whether the rumors are true or not, she's bound to be upset.

(b) Avoid her 'til you can find out what really happened.

55

(c) Support her, but you can't help feeling really embarrassed when people ask you about it.

4 There's a new girl at school. She's very cool, very nice, and a lot of fun. And she wants to hang with you. But there's one problem—she doesn't get along with your best friend. What do you do?
(a) Blow off your best friend.
(b) Invite your best friend along, although it will get tense. Hey, you tried.
(c) Live by the Girl Scout adage: "Make new friends, but keep the old."

5 Your friend has decided to do a Walk-a-Thon to benefit a local charity. She begs you to sign up too, so you do. The day arrives and it's gray and rainy—the perfect day to sleep in. What do you do?
(a) Sleep in.
(b) Put on your happy face and bring an umbrella big enough for two.
(c) Go, but grumble the whole way.

Answer always, sometimes, or never to the following statements:

6 I cancel on friends at the last minute.

7 I show up late when I'm meeting friends.

8 I take out my bad moods on my friends.

9 How long have you known your best friend?
(a) At least two years.
(b) We held hands in the playpen (practically).
(c) You mean my best friend this week?

SCORING:

(1)	a=1	b=2	c=3
(2)	a=2	b=3	c=1
(3)	a=3	b=1	c=2
(4)	a=1	b=2	c=3
(5)	a=1	b=3	c=2
(6)	always=1	sometimes=2	never=3
(7)	always=1	sometimes=2	never=3
(8)	always=1	sometimes=2	never=3
(9)	a=2	b=3	c=1

If your score is:

22 - 27: TRUE-BLUE.
You are an excellent friend. You treat your buds well and you're as loyal as they come. Just make sure not to sell yourself short while you're looking out for everyone around you. You've got to be a good friend to yourself, too.

15 - 21: IN-BETWEEN.
You're getting there. Like most of us, you aren't the perfect friend all the time. Try thinking of your friends' feelings more often. You'll see how great the results are.

9 - 14: FAIR-WEATHER.
Maybe you need to give your friendship skills the once-over. Try being a little more supportive—have those tissues ready when someone needs a shoulder to cry on! Your friends will appreciate it, and with a different attitude you might even make some new ones!

HOW (DIS)ORGANIZED ARE YOU?

Is your life in perfect order—or total chaos? Are you somewhere in between? Just how organized are you?

1 **What does your closet look like?**
(a) Clothes arranged by type and further broken down by color.
(b) Stuff is on hangers, but there's no real pattern.
(c) Closet? My bedroom floor is so covered with clothes I can't even remember what color my carpet is.

2 **The best description of your locker is:**
(a) Crowded—but I know where everything is.
(b) Messy—I'm late for class every day because I can't find a thing.
(c) Systematic—it has plastic dividers so there is a section for each class.

3 **You miss class assignments:**
(a) Usually—I rarely complete an assignment on time.
(b) Only in dire circumstances.
(c) Never! My handy diary system keeps me on top of everything.

4 **True or false:**
When buying birthday cards for friends and family members I always go straight to the "belated" section.

5 **Do you spend a lot of time looking for lost things?**
(a) Every so often.
(b) Never.
(c) I spend at least ten minutes searching for something every morning.

6 Describe your schoolbooks:

(a) I have already managed to lose my math and science textbooks, and it's only first semester.

(b) My notebooks are color coded with my book covers.

(c) They are relatively neat—most have covers, and I have a notebook for each class.

7 Your sister asks for a pair of earrings you borrowed from her. What do you do?

(a) Tear your room apart, then realize they're in your ears.

(b) Reach over and pick them up off your night stand.

(c) Without batting an eyelash, tell her, "They're on the second shelf of my jewelry box on the left side."

SCORING:

(1)	a=3	b=2	c=1
(2)	a=2	b=1	c=3
(3)	a=1	b= 2	c=3
(4)	true=0	false=2	
(5)	a=2	b=3	c=1
(6)	a=1	b=3	c=2
(7)	a=1	b=2	c=3

If your score is:

16 - 20: NEAT FREAK.
You are extremely organized. Your locker, bedroom, appearance, etc. all get you the Good Housekeeping Seal of Approval. But while you may never lose anything or miss an assignment, you're probably a little too compulsive. Think about easing up.

11 - 15: NOBODY'S PERFECT.
You are just about average on the organizational scale. You don't get too crazy about things, and you don't let things slide too much either.

6 - 10: OINK, OINK.
You don't have an organized bone in your body. While you could kindly be called laid back, some people might think that you're lost in space! You don't have to be a drill sergeant, but try a little more organization and watch your life get less frustrating.

YOUR DIVIDED BRAIN

Which side of your brain controls YOU? Some scientists believe that we tend to use one side of the brain more than the other, and that being "right-brained" or "left-brained" can influence the way we feel, act, and learn. The left side of the brain handles math skills, logic, and your ability to talk and write. The right side controls non-verbal abilities, such as drawing. This side of your brain is imaginative, rather unorganized, and relies on feeling rather than logic. Take this true-or-false quiz to see which side of your brain you favor.

- I would rather read a book than draw a picture.
- I do much better in math class than art class.
- I always wear a wristwatch.
- I am hardly ever late.
- I make decisions based on careful thought, not because I have a hunch.
- When someone gives me directions, I like to have them written out rather than drawn for me.
- I like throwing things out.
- I squeeze toothpaste from the bottom of the tube.
- I try not to put things off.

If you answered "true" to most of these questions, you may be "left-brained"—logical, analytical, and practical.

If you answered "false" to most of these questions you may be more "right-brained"—artistic, intuitive, and creative.

WHEN IS TACT THE BEST TACTIC?

Your parents told you always to tell the truth—so do you? Even when your father asks if you really like the Donald Duck necklace he picked out especially for you on his business trip? Should you be brutally honest and perhaps hurt his feelings, or tell a big lie and risk getting kiddie jewelry on every major holiday? Or do you know how to be tactful? Take this quiz and find out.

1 **Your friend just tried out for the softball team and didn't make it. She's really not all that great, so you're not surprised. She, however, is pretty bummed. What do you say to her?**
(a) "They made a big mistake. You were the best."
(b) "That's too bad—I'm really sorry."
(c) "Well, you're better off. You probably would have spent the entire season riding the bench anyway."

2 **Your best friend just got a terrible haircut. She asks for your honest opinion. You tell her:**
(a) The truth—it looks like someone took a weed-whacker to her head.
(b) She looks great—and cross your fingers behind your back.
(c) Maybe she'll start a trend. It's a different and unusual look.

3 **Your mom likes to experiment in the kitchen and she's just created a new recipe—she calls it Goulash Surprise. You think it should be renamed Mold Spore Stew. When she asks you what you think, you tell her:**
(a) "Mmm, mmm, good," as you reach for a second helping and sneak it to the dog.
(b) "I cannot tell a lie, Mom. It really stinks."

(c) "It's not one of my favorites—you make so many other great dishes."

4 You just met your boyfriend's cousin for the first time. He's so cute he makes you weak in the knees. When your boyfriend asks you what you thought, you say:

(a) "Where have you been hiding that Greek god?"
(b) "I see good looks run in your family."
(c) "Frankly, he was kind of boring."

5 Your best friend lends you a book she says was totally amazing. You read it and think it's mindless drivel. She asks what you thought about it. You say:

(a) "It was mindless drivel."
(b) "I thought the Fabio cover was pretty cool."
(c) "It wasn't exactly my cup of tea."

6 A girl in your homeroom leans over and asks if she has too much makeup on. She looks like Bozo the Clown. You say:

(a) "No, you look great!"
(b) "That depends—is the circus in town?"
(c) "Maybe just a little," and hand her a tissue.

7 Your friend introduces you to her new boyfriend. He is loud, crude, and obnoxious. She seems completely oblivious. You:

(a) Let her find out for herself. If she ever does ask your opinion, you'll tell her he's not your type, but if he makes her happy...
(b) Take her aside and tell her he's a real loser—she can do much better.
(c) Tell her what a great guy he is.

8 A goofy but nice guy from school calls and asks you out. You are horrified at the very idea. You:

(a) Tell him you don't want to ruin your friendship by introducing the dating element.

(b) Say, "Uh, I have a boyfriend," and get off the phone quick before he can ask you who this imaginary beau is.

(c) Say, "Excuse me, but what planet are you from? *Me* date *you?*"

9 Your friend walks into school with a major zit between her eyes. It's so big you can see it from all the way down the hall. When she asks you if it's noticeable, you reply:

(a) "You mean your third eye?"

(b) "It's not that bad."

(c) "You have a zit? Imagine that. I didn't notice."

10 You're at a party with your new boyfriend of one week. He returns from a trip to the bathroom with his fly open. What do you do?

(a) Call out that playground favorite: "Afraid of heights? Your zipper is."

(b) Don't say a word. This is too mortifying for words.

(c) Lean over and whisper the news to him. He'll get over the brief embarrassment and probably appreciate your honesty.

11 A friend of yours just got dumped by her first serious boyfriend. In your humble opinion, he was nowhere near good enough for her. What do you say to console her?

(a) "I'm sure you'll get back together—he'll come around any day now."

(b) "You're much better off without him. He was a jerk anyway. Remember Tina's party? He totally came on to me while you were in the bathroom."

(c) Tell her you completely understand and then treat her to a funny movie—with all the popcorn and Sugar Babies you both can eat.

SCORING:

(1)	a=1	b=2	c=3
(2)	a=3	b=1	c=2
(3)	a=1	b=3	c=2
(4)	a=3	b=2	c=1
(5)	a=3	b=1	c=2
(6)	a=1	b=3	c=2
(7)	a=2	b=3	c=1
(8)	a=2	b=1	c=3
(9)	a=3	b=2	c=1
(10)	a=3	b=1	c=2
(11)	a=1	b=3	c=2

If your score is:

27 - 33: OUCH!

Maybe brutal honesty doesn't bother you, so you think your friends can take it, too. You're probably wrong. Lighten up a bit. There's a difference between telling the truth and hurting people's feelings.

18 - 26: THE DIPLOMAT.

You don't lie, but you know how to soften the blow and avoid a potentially painful situation. You realize sometimes the whole truth just isn't called for. Your friend doesn't need to know she's a bad softball player, she needs to know you sympathize with her. Your boyfriend knows what a stud his cousin is, he just wants to know you think he's pretty darned cute, too.

11 - 17: SUGAR-COATER.

You've gone beyond tactful. You're probably just anxious not to hurt or offend anybody. But you're overdoing it. Sometimes no answer at all is better than an obvious lie. And sometimes people ask you your opinion for a reason— they may really want your help and value your advice.

SUPERSTITION SMARTS

Do you know...what to do if a black cat crosses your path? Which part of a rabbit's anatomy is the most lucky? How many years of bad luck you could get if you break a mirror? Take this quiz and find out your superstition I.Q.!

1 **You're eating dinner at home, when you accidentally knock the saltshaker over. To avoid bad luck, what should you do?**
(a) Excuse yourself three times.
(b) Toss salt over your left shoulder.
(c) Spill the pepper next.

2 **When you pass a cemetery, to keep the evil spirits away you should always:**
(a) Pretend to cry for the recently departed.
(b) Run as fast as you can.
(c) Hold your breath.

3 **If your shoelace is untied, legend has it that:**
(a) Someone is talking about you.
(b) You will trip and fall.
(c) You can make three wishes.

4 **Complete this sentence: Step on a crack...**
(a) Buy a new backpack.
(b) Break your mother's back.
(c) Little ducks go quack.

5 **You bite your tongue while you are eating. What does this signify?**
(a) That you shouldn't be taking such big mouthfuls.
(b) You recently told a lie.
(c) You will be kissed soon.

6 **Pair up the following superstitions:**
(a) Itchy foot
(b) Cold hands
(c) Nose itches
(and you rub it)
(d) Itchy right hand
(e) Itchy left hand
(f) Itchy right ear
(g) Itchy left ear

(1) You'll get a letter.
(2) Someone is saying something bad about you.
(3) You'll receive money.
(4) You'll take a trip.
(5) You are a generous person.
(6) Someone is saying nice things about you.
(7) You'll lose money.

7 **Which of the following will bring rain?**
(a) Shoes on the wrong feet.
(b) Picking pansies.
(c) Stepping on a spider.
(d) Squashing a toad.
(e) Forgetting to milk the cow.

8 **You tell one of your friends, "I've never gotten less than a B+ on any of my report cards." What should you say next to make sure you never will?**
(a) "So be it."
(b) "And proud of it."
(c) "Knock on wood."

9 **If you tell a lie, what is the only way to make it not count?**
(a) Say, "That was a lie I just told you."
(b) Cross your fingers.
(c) Bow your head.

10 **For good luck all month long, the first thing you should say on the first day of the month is:**
(a) "Good morning."
(b) "Broccoli."
(c) "Rabbit."

11 And last but not least, which is the worst kind of bad luck there is?

(a) Opening an umbrella indoors.

(b) Putting a hat on a bed.

(c) Three people making a bed together.

SCORING:

(Score two points for each correct answer, including the matching column. For 7 and 11 score points only if you get all three.)

(1)	b
(2)	c
(3)	a
(4)	b
(5)	b
(6)	a-4, b-5, c-1, d-3, e-7, f-6, g-2
(7)	b,c,d
(8)	c
(9)	b
(10)	c
(11)	a,b, and c

If your score is:

24 - 34: GENIUS.
Have you been hanging out with the Old Wives? How else to explain why you know so many of their tales? Just don't take them too seriously. They're just for fun—really!

12 - 22: AVERAGE.
You have a pretty good knowledge of superstitions. In fact, you could be a superstition expert before you know it— knock on wood!

0 - 10: DUNCE.
You wouldn't know what to do with a four-leaf clover if one bit you on the nose!!!

ARE YOU SPOILED ROTTEN?

Are you Daddy's little princess? Do you get everything and anything you want no matter how outrageous it may be? Find out just how spoiled you really are.

1 Is there anything you daydream about owning someday?

(a) A car.

(b) A pair of shoes that match.

(c) Oh...Buckingham Palace, the Hope Diamond...

2 What kind of chores do you do around the house?

(a) Cook dinner every night and pay the bills.

(b) Walk the dog, keep my room neat, clear the table.

(c) Chores? Oh, please!

3 Do you get an allowance?

(a) Yes—based on the chores I've done for the week.

(b) Yes—just for being sweet little old me.

(c) No—I pay my parents to raise me.

4 Have you ever had a job?

(a) Yes, I work full-time, seven nights a week, in addition to school.

(b) Yes, an after-school job.

(c) Work? I might break my nails.

5 When it comes to family vacations:

(a) I'm never invited along. I stay at home to watch the dog.

(b) Everyone goes where I want to go. (And I think we'll go to Disneyland for the eleventh year in a row!)

(c) Everyone decides as a family.

6 Complete this sentence: When I get my driver's license...

(a) Daddy's buying me a convertible with vanity plates that read SPOILED.

(b) I'll borrow the family car.

(c) Forget about it—I don't even have a bicycle!

7 You really want Pearl Jam tickets for your birthday. You end up getting:

(a) Galoshes and long underwear—practicality first.

(b) Pearl Jam tickets.

(c) Eddie Vedder singing "Happy Birthday" to you, and backstage passes.

SCORING:

(1)	a=2	b=1	c=3
(2)	a=1	b=2	c=3
(3)	a=2	b=3	c=1
(4)	a=1	b=2	c=3
(5)	a=1	b=3	c=2
(6)	a=3	b=2	c=1
(7)	a=1	b=2	c=3

If your score is:

17 - 21: PAMPERED PRINCESS.
You are spoiled rotten—to the core. You are over-indulged, mollycoddled, a pampered princess, you name it! Enjoy yourself, dear, you've got it made!

12 - 16: REGULAR "JO."
You are well-adjusted, unspoiled, and perfectly normal in every way!

7 - 11: INDENTURED SERVANT.
There are Child Labor Laws against this sort of thing! Put down that scrub brush and contact your local social worker—pronto!

ARE YOU A LEADER?

Are you the leader of the pack, or just another sheep in the flock? Do you take the bull by the horns, or do you let someone else grab all the glory? Take this quiz and check out your leadership potential.

Answer always, sometimes, or never to the following statements:

1 You volunteer in class, even if you're not absolutely certain you are correct.

2 You withhold your opinion if you know that someone may disagree with you.

True or false:

3 The thought of running for student office makes you break into a cold sweat.

4 It would be great to be picked captain of a team you're on.

5 Your friends think that miniature golfing is for losers. There's nothing that pleases you more on a fine summer day than putting a bright pink ball past a spinning windmill. What's the outcome?

(a) You decide they're right—miniature golfing is for geeks.

(b) You continue with your guilty little pleasure—and just keep it under wraps.

(c) You convince your pals to give it a try—they might just like it.

6 All of your friends have similar hairstyles. You see a cool new look in a magazine—but you're not sure what your friends will think. What do you do?

(a) Conduct an informal poll to check your friends' opinions.

(b) Forget about it. If one of your friends didn't get this 'do first, it must be goofy.

(c) Go for it. You don't follow trends—you set them.

7 All your friends hate the new health teacher. She's been nice to you, and you like her. They're trashing her at lunchtime. You say:

(a) "You're right, she is kinda freaky."

(b) Nothing. Your friends might think you're weird.

(c) "You guys are all wrong—she's really cool."

8 Go back in time. You're in the second grade, and a bunch of your classmates are picking on the boy who wears weird clothes and eats paste. Which kid are you?

(a) The one who feels really awful, but doesn't say a word.

(b) The one who confronts the ringleader and forces her to apologize.

(c) The one who joins in because you're glad you're not the one being picked on.

9 Your teacher just made a statement in class you know is wrong. What do you do?

(a) Raise your hand and initiate a debate.

(b) Go to her after class and tell her what you think.

(c) Disagree with a teacher? No way.

10 You are out hiking with some friends on a trail you've been on once before. You come to a fork in the road. The sign has fallen down. One of your friends insists that the trail you want is to the right. You're almost positive it's the other way. Do you say anything?

(a) Yes. But not until you're absolutely positive you're lost—which is a half hour onto the wrong trail.

(b) No. You must be wrong. Your friend knows where she's going.

(c) Yes. You speak up immediately.

11 Your class has been broken up into groups to do a report. It's painfully obvious that your group is going nowhere fast. Someone needs to take charge, or you will all get a big fat F. What do you do?

(a) Sit back and hope that someone takes charge—soon!

(b) Suggest a group vote to elect a leader.

(c) Whip out a notebook and a pen and start assigning duties.

12 You really think that your school should have a rock-climbing club. What is your course of action?

(a) Get the ball rolling, pronto.

(b) Bring it up with some students who are also into it and hope that one of them will get the club going.

(c) Don't do anything, but keep thinking you should.

SCORING:

(1)	always=3	sometimes=2	never=1
(2)	always=1	sometimes=2	never=3
(3)	true=0	false=2	
(4)	true=2	false=0	
(5)	a=1	b=2	c=3
(6)	a=2	b=1	c=3
(7)	a=1	b=2	c=3
(8)	a=2	b=3	c=1
(9)	a=3	b=2	c=1
(10)	a=2	b=1	c=3
(11)	a=1	b=2	c=3
(12)	a=3	b=2	c=1

If your score is:

27 - 34: GO-GETTER.
You are not afraid to take charge of a situation. You know what you want and how to get it. Your confidence and initiative are admirable. Just be careful to pay attention to other people's wishes, too.

18 - 26: HOLDING BACK.
You're ready to put yourself forward when you feel strongly about something. That's great. But sometimes you sit back when you really have something to contribute. Maybe you're afraid of being in the limelight? Try speaking up even if an issue isn't major for you.

10 - 17: CROWD PLEASER.
You tend to go along with the crowd just to fit in. You're being unfair to yourself. Take a deep breath and stand up for what you believe. You may bring a new perspective to the situation.

THE NAME GAME

Who do you think would be more likely to ace an exam—Agatha or Candi? Which girl would be the better cheerleader? Your name can really influence how people think of you. In a recent study, people were given a list of names and asked to imagine what each person would be like. It turned out nicknames, like "Kate" or "Susie," suggested popularity and cheerfulness. "Katherine" or "Susan," on the other hand, gave the impression of greater success. "Heather" was rated a sexy name, while "Holly" seemed friendly. In another study, people looked at the same photograph of a woman and rated her much more attractive if she was labelled "Jennifer" instead of "Gertrude." Some psychologists say your name can even influence the way you feel about yourself.

So think about it. Do you let names influence you? Is your name sending a message?

LET'S GET PHYSICAL

Do you prefer to exercise your body, or your right to do nothing at all? Are you a fitness freak, or a couch potato?

1 Which choice is closest to your typical Saturday morning?
(a) Cartoons and Cap'n Crunch on the couch.
(b) Sports, shopping, whatever's on the agenda for the day.
(c) Up at the crack of dawn to train for an upcoming triathalon.

2 When you wake up on a typical school morning, you feel:
(a) Like it's time for a nap.
(b) Like you're ready to conquer the world!
(c) Like you'll be fine once you take a shower.

3 How do you feel about gym class?
(a) It can be fun.
(b) It's the high point of my day.
(c) It's pure torture.

4 How often do you watch television?
(a) When something good is on.
(b) Constantly—you watch even those infomercials.
(c) You watch the Olympics every two years—that's about it.

5 The last time you broke a sweat was:
(a) During your last marathon.
(b) While trying to open a bag of Cheez Doodles.
(c) While you were playing softball with your friends.

6 Which choice best describes your exercise regime?

(a) You try to do some sort of physical activity a couple of times a week.

(b) Running, biking, swimming. That's on Monday...

(c) Exercise? You run only if someone is chasing you.

7 Your typical dinner consists of:

(a) Fast food all the way.

(b) You try to follow the food pyramid.

(c) Gotta load up on those carbs!

SCORING:

(1)	a=1	b=2	c=3
(2)	a=1	b=3	c=2
(3)	a=2	b=3	c=1
(4)	a=2	b=1	c=3
(5)	a=3	b=1	c=2
(6)	a=2	b=3	c=1
(7)	a=1	b=2	c=3

If your score is:

17 - 21: FITNESS FANATIC.
You are a super-jock! Just be careful not to burn yourself out.

12 - 16: JOGGING ALONG.
You try to keep in good shape and think it's important to take care of yourself. Keep up the healthy eating and exercising habits!

7 - 11: OUT OF THE RUNNING.
Hey, Ms. Couch Potato, wake up—it's time to get moving!

MISS MANNERS

Do you always remember to say "please" and "thank you"? To say "Gesundheit" when someone sneezes? What kind of manners do you have?

1 You are at the mall with your aunt when you run into two girls you know from school. You:

(a) Yap away, leaving your aunt standing uncomfortably behind you.

(b) Talk for a while, then say, "Oh yeah, this is my aunt."

(c) Introduce her right away and try to include her in the conversation.

2 You answer the phone. It's your older brother's new girlfriend. He is unable to take the call at that moment. What do you say?

(a) "Sorry, he can't come to the phone right now, can I have him call you right back?"

(b) "Ummmm...he's not here."

(c) "He's going to the bathroom."

3 It's your birthday, and you've just unwrapped a gift from your Great-Aunt Matilda—a framed print of The New Kids on the Block. What do you say?

(a) "Funny, Aunt M! Now where's my real gift?"

(b) "New Kids—how quaint!"

(c) "Thank you very much."

4 You are out to dinner at a fancy restaurant with a friend and her parents. There is an array of utensils in front of you and you're totally confused. What do you do?

(a) Pick one fork and use it the entire evening. This is way too confusing.

(b) Follow what your friend's mother does. You're sure she knows what she's doing.

(c) Order only food you can eat with your hands. You're having lobster for dinner!

5 You are walking down the street and you and another person accidentally collide. What do you say?

(a) "Excuse me."

(b) Nothing.

(c) "Why don't you look where you're going?"

6 You are hurrying into the post office. Just as you approach the door, you notice a slow-moving old lady several paces behind you. You:

(a) Hold the door for her patiently.

(b) Hold the door, but you're pretty annoyed by the time she finally gets there.

(c) Speed up so you won't feel obligated to be the designated doorman.

7 You are invited to a birthday party. The invitation requests you to RSVP a week before the party. You:

(a) Wait 'til a day or two before to call—you never know when something better might come up.

(b) Never call. You'll decide if you're going the day of the party. Calling is just an unnecessary formality anyway.

(c) Call as soon as you know whether you're going or not.

SCORING:

(1)	a=1	b=2	c=3
(2)	a=3	b=2	c=1
(3)	a=1	b=2	c=3
(4)	a=2	b=3	c=1
(5)	a=3	b=2	c=1
(6)	a=3	b=2	c=1
(7)	a=2	b=1	c=3

If your score is:

17 - 21: PERFECTLY POLITE.
Well, Miss Manners, somebody certainly taught you the rules of etiquette!

12 - 16: ETIQUETTELY CHALLENGED.
Your manners could definitely use a bit of brushing up. Check out a copy of an etiquette book from the library. You may feel more confident about yourself if you know the right thing to do in even the most awkward social situation.

7 - 11: EXCUSE YOU!
Were you raised in a barn? Okay, some polite conventions are just plain silly, but for the most part, manners are about treating other people with respect. And, seriously, you may be putting people off with your lack of courtesy.

Which type of guy appeals to you the most? The athletic type? The sensitive soul? The funny guy? The boy with an attitude? Take this quiz and discover...

WHO'S YOUR MR. RIGHT?

1 **What do you look for in a guy?**
(a) Big muscles.
(b) Artistic talent.
(c) Good sense of humor.
(d) Tattoos—plenty of 'em.

2 **What do you like to wear on a date?**
(a) Jeans and a T-shirt.
(b) Long, flowing skirts.
(c) Something bright and cheerful.
(d) Black leather.

3 **Which type of movie would you most like to see?**
(a) Anything to do with sports.
(b) A romantic foreign film.
(c) A comedy.
(d) Action.

4 **Which guy would you be most likely to have a crush on?**
(a) The guy in your gym class with the nice legs.
(b) The guy in your English class who knows all of those Emily Dickinson poems by heart.
(c) The guy with the funniest answers in class.
(d) The guy who tells the teacher off and spends all his time in detention.

5 **The most romantic thing a guy could do for you would be:**
(a) Score you a touchdown.
(b) Write you a poem.

(c) Tell you a funny joke when you're feeling down.

(d) Carve your name in his arm.

6 What would you most like to do on a date?

(a) Go to a hockey game.

(b) Go to a symphony concert in the park.

(c) Go to a stand-up comedy club.

(d) Go for a ride on his Harley.

7 What do you do in your spare time?

(a) Shoot hoops.

(b) Write in your diary.

(c) Watch old Monty Python movies.

(d) Tune the engine on the family car.

SCORING:

Mostly A's.

You seem to go for rugged, sports-minded jocks—and the buff bods sure don't hurt either!

Mostly B's.

Your heart flip-flops for the romantic, sensitive type with a poet's soul. You like red roses, picnics in the park, candlelit dinners, and holding hands.

Mostly C's.

It's the class-clown type for you. As far as you're concerned, the most romantic thing in the world is a good laugh.

Mostly D's.

You can't help it—your heart beats double-time for the rebellious type. A cool guy with an attitude is definitely your Mr. Right.